MW00904342

Nana's Little Stories

Written by Patricia Rogers
Illustrated by Yoko Matsuoka

First Edition

PAGE PUBLISHING, INC.
New York, NY

First originally published by Page Publishing, Inc. 2015

ISBN 978-1-62838-623-3 (pbk)
ISBN 978-1-62838-624-0 (digital)
ISBN 978-1-62838-625-7 (hardcover)

Printed in the United States of America

To Mia and Dylan, who asked me to write down some of my stories,
and to Cooper who listens to them and says, "Again?"
And to darling little Peyton, who has just joined our family.

Love, Nana

The Baby Bat and His Cave

Once upon a time, there was a baby bat. His name was Little Bat. He lived in a cave with his mommy and daddy. When he was really little, he couldn't go outside of the cave because it wasn't safe. But as he grew, his mommy and daddy taught him how to fly around the cave, which was their home, so he would learn how to be safe when he finally went outside. It was very dark in the cave. In fact, the baby bat couldn't see anything inside the cave because it was so dark. But that was okay because bats can find their way in the dark with special "radar." They can tell, even in the dark, where things are so they won't run into them. It is a very special talent. Besides, bats go outside all night to hunt and return to the cave during the day to sleep, so it helps to have the cave dark.

When the Little Bat got bigger, his mommy and daddy took him out into the big world outside the cave. But they were always very close so he would be safe while he learned to fly. Little by little, he got better at flying, and little by little, he got braver about being in the big world outside the cave. There was much more light outside the cave, and that made it easier for him to explore the big world.

One day, the Little Bat wasn't a baby anymore. His mommy and daddy told him that he was old enough to fly outside in the big world all by himself. He was a little scared, but Mommy and Daddy said it would be okay, so off he went.

It was so much fun! He flew high and low and up and down and in circles! It felt so good to be able to fly anywhere he wanted to and be big enough to do it on his own. So every night, he would follow his mommy and daddy and the other bats out of the cave. Then he would go off on his own to explore and have fun.

One night, he was flying quite far from the cave when he spotted something on the ground. It was glowing and golden. He had no idea what it was, so he decided to swoop down and take a closer look. He flew lower, and sure enough, it was a little walnut shell that contained some golden, glowing, sparkly dust. Now he was really curious! He swooped lower and lower until he thought it was safe to stop on the ground next to the walnut shell and take a closer look.

It was amazing! He had never seen anything like it before. The dust inside the shell glowed and sparkled. It was beautiful! He decided that his mommy and daddy, and all the other bats that lived in his cave should see this wonderful glowing sparkly dust.

So he picked up the walnut shell and took it back to the cave, just in time for all the bats to see before they went to sleep for the day. When he got there, his mommy and daddy and all his cousins and family were there. On the way into the cave, he accidentally spilled a tiny bit of the golden dust.

All of a sudden, the entire cave was filled with wonderful light and a golden glow. For the first time, the bats could see what the inside of their cave home looked like.

It was the most wondrous thing they had ever seen. Beautiful colors were everywhere. There were reds, oranges, golden browns, cream, blue, black—more colors than you could describe. Then there were the formations. Stalactites, stalagmites, bacon forms, shields, huge towers the size of big buildings, and a trickle of water at the bottom that sparkled with the light. All the bats were truly surprised. It was so beautiful! And it was the first time they ever knew that they lived in such a beautiful place.

All the bats came over to the little bat and thanked him for bringing the dust to the cave. They all decided that they would keep the dust, and once in awhile, they would spill a little bit so they could see their wonderful home.

Well, Little Bat knew that the dust wouldn't last forever. So the next night, he flew back to the place he found the walnut shell. He thought that maybe he could find some more. What he found surprised him even more.

There on the ground was a little ground squirrel. And he was crying so hard! Little Bat flew down and asked the little squirrel what was wrong and why was he crying so hard. The little squirrel told Little Bat that he had lost something that was very special. He told him that he had lost a walnut shell filled with magical golden dust. It was a very magical dust that could help make sick squirrels better. His grandmother was sick, and he was bringing it to her to make her better. He had stopped to rest and fell asleep, and when he woke up, the shell and the magical dust was gone.

Now Little Bat had a problem. He knew that the little squirrel was talking about the shell and dust he found. Should he keep the dust for his family so they could see their beautiful cave whenever they wanted to or should he give it back to the little squirrel so he could help his grandmother or any other sick squirrels? He thought very hard.

Then he realized what he should do. He told the little squirrel that he had found the dust and taken it back to his cave. He asked the little squirrel if he could keep it one more night so his family could see the wondrous cave one more time and then Little Bat would bring it back to the little squirrel.

That made the little squirrel so happy! He jumped up and down and hugged Little Bat. "Yes," he said, "that would be perfect." Little Bat went back to the cave and told his mommy and daddy what had happened. They all agreed that he had done the right thing.

That night, all the bats saw the beautiful cave. They were very happy to see it one more time, and they all thought that Little Bat made the right choice.

The next day, Little Bat took the walnut shell and the dust back to the spot where the little squirrel was waiting. The little squirrel was so happy to have the magical dust back. He jumped up and down and hugged Little Bat. He also knew that Little Bat did a very nice and kind thing to tell him about the dust and to bring it back so it would help his family

He told Little Bat that he was so thankful and that his family was so thankful that once a year, he would leave a little of the dust right on the spot where they were so Little Bat could take it back to the cave. So once a year, Little Bat would fly to that spot, pick up a shell with a little bit of the dust and take it back to the cave so all the bats could see how beautiful their home was.

And Little Bat and the little squirrel were friends forever.

THE END

Little Wolf and Little Fox

Once upon a time, there was a little wolf and a little fox that lived in the forest very near each other. When they were little cubs and just learning about the world, they happened to find each other while they were out playing in a meadow. They had so much fun together. They would run fast, chase butterflies, chase dandelion seeds when the wind would blow them, and they would chase each other! They played hide and seek, which was their favorite, because they got to explore the surrounding forest. Soon they knew where every empty stump, cave, rock, hiding places, and all the parts of the forest. They had such a good time that they would meet in their favorite meadow and play and play. Their mothers would have to round them up when it was time to come inside for dinner. But each morning, as soon as they could, they would run to the meadow and play.

One morning, they went to the meadow and decided to find another spot. They had heard about a stream nearby. It was a pretty hot day, and they thought that if they could find the stream, they could splash around and cool off at the same time. So off they went and sure enough, they had not gone very far when they heard the water. They raced to the sound as fast as they could go.

When the got there, the little wolf, who was leading the way, stopped suddenly. The little fox was right behind him, so when Little Wolf stopped, Little Fox smashed right into Little Wolf and they both tumbled right into the stream! They rolled in the water, and when they finally stood up, Little Fox said, "Why did you stop so suddenly, Little Wolf?" Little Wolf replied, "Because I heard something." As you know, wolves have excellent hearing and can hear almost anything. "It was coming from across the stream, from behind that tree."

The stream was not very deep, so Little Wolf and Little Fox carefully trotted across the water to the other side. Sure enough, they both heard something. It sounded like crying, but they weren't sure. Now foxes are known for their very sharp eyesight. Little Fox spotted something hidden in the bushes.

"I see something!" Little Fox said to Little Wolf.

"Where?" asked Little Wolf.

"Right there by that dark green bush with the berries on it," replied Little Fox.

"That's where the sound is coming from too." Little Wolf was starting to get excited. They had found something new in the forest.

Little Fox and Little Wolf carefully walked over to the spot behind the bushes. They didn't know what to expect. When they got to the spot, they were very surprised to see a baby bear crying and sad.

"What's the matter, Baby Bear?" they both asked.

"I'm sad because I've lost my mommy," the little bear said. "We were out finding berries, and I thought I heard bees nearby and went to see if there was some honey. When I tried to find my way back to my mommy, I got lost. I don't know where she is."

With that, the baby bear cried harder.

Little Fox and Little Wolf weren't quite sure what to do. Then they had an idea.

"Let's play in the meadow until your mommy comes back. All the animals know where the meadow is, and your mommy is sure to look there for you."

The baby bear stopped sniffling and thought for a minute.

"That sounds like a good idea," he said.

So off the three of them went. When they were back in the meadow, they played tag and chased butterflies and each other. Baby Bear quite forgot about being sad and worried. They played until the sun started to go down. Then Baby Bear realized it was time to go home. He started to cry again.

This time Little Fox and Little Wolf looked at each other. They had been quite sure that Mommy Bear would have come to the meadow by now. Little Wolf had an idea. Since he had very good ears and Little Fox had very good eyes, maybe they could work together and find Baby Bear's home.

They explained this to Baby Bear and told him not to cry because they would help and find his mommy. So Little Wolf pricked his ears up and Little Fox looked all the way around the meadow. At the far end of the meadow, Little Fox saw a path they had never gone to before. They decided to follow it and see where it went. When they got to the path, Little Wolf heard something. It was a strange sound. It sounded like a bellow. "*Arrrgh, arrgh.*"

The little animals and Baby Bear went toward the sound. It got louder. Little Fox used his very good eyes and saw that not too far away was a hill with a cave in it. They got closer and closer to the cave, and the sound got louder and louder. When they got to the bottom of the hill, the sound was very loud.

"That's my mommy!" shouted Baby Bear. "Mommy, Mommy," he yelled.

At the mouth of the cave, a very large bear appeared.

"Is that you, Baby Bear?" called Mommy Bear.

"Yes, it's me!" shouted Baby Bear.

Mommy Bear rushed down the hill and picked up Baby Bear and gave him a big hug. She was so glad to see him, and he was so glad to see her. They just kept hugging. When they stopped hugging, Mommy Bear looked down to see Little Wolf and Little Fox quietly slipping away.

"Baby Bear, are the wolf and the fox the ones who brought you back?" she asked.

"Yes, Mommy, they found you for me." Baby Bear smiled.

Mommy Bear said to Little Wolf and Little Fox, "I want to thank you for bringing Baby Bear back to me."

Both Little Wolf and Little Fox smiled, well, as much as animals can smile. Then they knew it was time to go home, so they said, "You are very welcome, and if Baby Bear ever gets lost again, come to the meadow and find us. We'll help you find him."

Now, Little Wolf and Little Fox and Baby Bear are all grown up, but they still remember the day they had so much fun in the meadow and helped a baby bear find his mommy.

THE END

The Mistake

Once upon a time, there was a little bird. He lived in a nest with his mommy and daddy and their family in a big shady oak tree. It was so big that Little Bird could hop all day in the tree and never have to leave it. He very much liked the big tree that was his home and his parents were very glad to have him close by where they knew he would be safe.

The tree his family lived in was close to a little town. Every year, on the other side of town, there was a fair that came to town. Little Bird had never seen it, but he had heard about it. There were so many things to see and do at the fair that it made Little Bird dizzy to think about it. All the other birds told Little Bird about the fair. There were special treats to eat—peanuts and cotton candy. There were rides that were loads of fun. There was a big fountain where birds could swim. But most of all, the one thing that every one of the birds talked about were the Flying Bluebirds. They put on the most amazing show. First, they were beautiful to look at. They had deep blue feathers with red tummies and were so pretty. Then they would fly together. They would fly alone and dive for flowers and then go back up again. They could make pictures in the air by flying together in a formation. They were dazzling! They were spectacular! They were the most wonderful, talented group of birds anyone had ever seen. Little Bird couldn't wait until he was old enough to go to the fair and see the Flying Bluebirds.

As time went by, Little Bird got bigger. One day, he was big enough to learn how to fly. His mommy and daddy took him to one of the lowest branches, so if he fell while he was trying to learn how to fly, he wouldn't be hurt. He practiced and practiced, taking off, landing, and flying around his nest until he got the hang of it. He was getting pretty good at it.

His uncle, Uncle Bird, told Little Bird that if he got to be good enough at flying by the time the fair came to town. Uncle Bird would take Little Bird to see the Flying Bluebirds. Mommy and Daddy Bird couldn't take Little Bird because they had more baby birds to watch in the nest.

Little Bird was so excited! The fair was in only one week. He tried harder and harder to learn to fly well. He practiced taking off; he practiced landing. He practiced gliding. He practiced going up and going down. Finally, he was doing so well that Uncle Bird said Little Bird was good enough to go to the fair and see the Famous Flying Bluebirds the very next day.

Little Bird couldn't wait. The day before he went to the fair went so slowly. Not even practicing flying would make it go faster. Finally, it was dinner time, and the sky started to go dark. The next morning was the fair!

When the sun came up the next morning, Little Bird had breakfast, and Uncle Bird came to get him. "Time to go to the fair and see the Famous Flying Bluebirds." Uncle Bird flew up and said to Little Bird, "Follow me." Off they went.

They flew up into the sky, and after a little while, they saw the village. Little Bird knew that the fair was on the other side of town. So they flew over the town and got to the other side, but there was nothing there.

"Where's the fair?" asked Little Bird.

"It should be right here," answered his uncle. "Wait here and I'll go ask. Maybe we got the wrong spot."

FAIR-
GROUND
CLOSED

So Little Bird waited and waited and waited some more. Finally, Uncle Bird returned and hung his head down low.

"I have some bad news, Little Bird," said Uncle Bird. "The fair ended yesterday. The fair and the Famous Flying Bluebirds are gone. I'm very sorry, but I made a mistake."

Little Bird couldn't believe his ears. No fair? No Famous Flying Bluebirds? It had to be wrong.

"Are you sure?" asked Little Bird.

"Yes, I am sure. This is where the fair would be if it was still here. I got the days mixed up, and we have missed it. I made a big mistake."

Little Bird burst into tears. "You told me you would take me!" he shouted. "I worked so hard on my flying. You promised!"

Little Bird was crying and yelling. He was mad and sad. Uncle Birds felt terrible because he had promised Little Bird, and he made a huge mistake. Uncle Bird didn't know what else to do, so they flew back to the nest in the oak tree.

When they got there, Little Bird flopped right into the nest and started stamping his feet and crying, "You promised me I would see the Famous Flying Bluebirds!"

Uncle Bird explained to Mommy and Daddy Bird what had happened. He felt awful and didn't know what to do. Mommy and Daddy Bird listened, and they also felt very bad that Little Bird was so disappointed.

Then Daddy Bird started to speak very softly to Little Bird, "Little Bird, we know how upset you are about missing the fair and the Famous Flying Bluebirds. We all feel terrible about this, but it was a mistake."

"Uncle Bird promised," wailed Little Bird, crying harder.

"Yes, he did, but he got the days mixed up and made a mistake. This is what you need to know about mistakes," said Daddy Bird.

"Mistakes happen. They happen to everyone. The thing to remember is that no one makes mistakes on purpose. Uncle Bird didn't mix up the days on purpose. He didn't disappoint you on purpose. It was a mistake."

"What do you do with a mistake?" Mommy Bird asked kindly.

"I don't know," sniffed Little Bird. He wasn't crying so loudly now.

“What you do with a mistake is make it a lesson. All of us make mistakes, but the trick is to learn from them. You might make other mistakes, but you won’t make the same mistake twice. That’s the key. Learn from your mistakes and don’t repeat them. Your uncle is very sorry you were disappointed, but the next time the fair comes to town, no one in this family will get the days mixed up, that’s for sure. We will all learn from this mistake. So dry your eyes, Little Bird. Mommy has made your favorite supper, and you will see the Famous Flying Bluebirds the next time.” Mommy gave Little Bird a hug. Then Uncle Bird gave Little Bird a hug.

Little Bird felt better. He understood now that even though he was disappointed, he learned how to fly way faster and way better than he would have without thinking about the fair.

So everyone in the big oak tree spent the next year being very busy with the business of being a bird. And sure enough, the next year, when the fair came to town, Little Bird, his uncle, and the whole family went to the fair and saw the Famous Flying Bluebirds.

It was a blast!

THE END

The Little Trolley

Once upon a time, there was a little electric trolley that lived in an amusement park. He wasn't very big, but he was shiny and very well maintained. His conductor made sure that he was washed and polished every day. He had bright green paint with polished brass trim and a spotless white top where his antennae were attached to the electric lines.

Every day he would go back and forth across the park. His trip wasn't a long one, but he did his best and tried very hard to make sure his ride went very smoothly so his passengers would enjoy it. His conductor would ring his bell and pull on the whistle cord so everyone knew when he was coming. People would get on at one end and get off at the other end. Usually, people rode on him when they were tired of walking across the park. And there was one little boy who came often to the park and rode the trolley several times each time he and his parents visited. This little boy always had a big smile when he rode the trolley.

Now this park was quite big and had many rides for the visitors besides the little trolley. There were fast roller coaster rides and high swinging rides and rides that went into tunnels and were scary. There were boat rides that went past very pretty sites. There were merry-go-rounds with beautiful painted horses. There were cars that drove very fast, and swinging rides that went back and forth.

The park always had a lot of people when it was open; and they all loved these fast, loud, swinging, scary rides. The park was always very loud with people laughing and yelling and screaming with all the fun and excitement. All the time that the park was open, the trolley went back and forth from one end of the park to the other. His ride wasn't fast or scary or dark. It was just a simple ride from one end of the park to the other.

The little trolley thought that his ride was fine until one night, when the park was closed, he heard some of the other rides talking.

"I'm the fastest ride," said the Big Roller Coaster. "There are long lines for me every day. The people can't wait to take my fast scary ride. They shout in delight and always say that my ride is the best. I am the best ride." He beamed with pride.

"Well, I'm the highest ride," said Giant Ferris Wheel. "When people take my ride they get to the highest place in the park. They can see the whole park and everything around it when they ride on me. They all say that I am quite the biggest Ferris wheel they have ever seen. I am the best ride."

"I'm the newest ride, and I go very fast," said Racing Car. "I'm brand new and shiny, and when they built my ride, they made it the most spectacular of all the other rides. There is always the longest line in the park for me." Just to prove his point, he revved up his engine, and true enough, he sounded very powerful. "I am the best ride."

“Well, I’m the scariest ride,” said Haunted Train. “I go into the dark and people see ghosts, goblins, and lots of scary things on my ride. Visitors come from everywhere because they have all heard about my scary ride. What’s more, you have to be a certain age even to ride with me. I am the best ride.”

“I am the most exciting ride,” said Rafting Ride. “People know that when they ride my ride, they will get very wet. But they do it anyway because they know it will be so exciting. They feel very brave and laugh and yell a lot while they are on my ride. So I must be the best.”

“I am the most beautiful and serene ride,” said Pretty Boat. “After the people ride on you, they come to me because they know that they will go quietly through pretty scenery and see wonderful sights that make them smile. They can relax and have a lovely time with their family and friends. You can’t beat that. I am the best.”

All this time Little Trolley said nothing. He hadn't really thought about who was the best ride. He just did his job and enjoyed every one of his trips back and forth through the park. The other rides looked over to him and asked, "What, exactly, do you do?"

Little Trolley replied, "I go from one end of the park to the other. And I do it every day. People who get tired of walking can ride on me. I stop at places so they can get on and off." He shrugged. "That's what I do."

All the other rides laughed at him. "What a boring life you have!" they said. "You aren't fast or scary or powerful or high or exciting or the newest and you don't go by beautiful scenery. Why, you're barely a ride at all."

Then they went on to chat about other things. Little Trolley felt very sad. He knew he wasn't a very special ride, but he liked what he did, and he liked helping people when they got tired. True, there was never a long line for his ride, but everyone said "Thank you" when they got off.

The next day, when the park opened, the first passenger to get on the Little Trolley was a little boy and his parents. The little boy looked at Little Trolley and smiled his biggest smile. Little Trolley thought he recognized the boy, and sure enough, he did. This little boy came to the park often with his mommy and daddy, and they always rode the trolley.

The conductor had noticed that morning that Little Trolley wasn't running his best, so he had double checked his motor and had given him an extra polish so he looked his best. But the conductor could tell something was off.

When the little boy and his parents got on the trolley, the little boy said, "All aboard!" The conductor looked down at the little boy and said, "Do you like the trolley ride?

"Oh yes!" said the little boy. "It is my favorite ride in the park."

"Really?" said the conductor.

"Yes yes," said the little boy. "He is so shiny and beautiful, and he does such a good job of going along his tracks. And I love his bells and whistle. He does the best job in the park of taking care of his passengers. I can't think of any ride better than this. I could ride on him forever."

"Well, my goodness," exclaimed the conductor. "Would you like to ring the bell and pull the whistle cord?"

The little boy's eyes lit up and his smile got even bigger. His daddy lifted him up because he was too little to reach the bell and whistle. He rang the bell and pulled the whistle and laughed. Then he did an extraordinary thing, he hugged the trolley's steering wheel!

Little Trolley couldn't believe it! He had never dreamed that he could be that special to anyone. But here was one of his passengers who thought he was the best. With that, he started his ride. He now knew that he didn't have to be the fastest or the newest or the scariest or the most beautiful. He just needed to be the best that he was, and his riders would love him.

THE END

The Halloween Cat!

Once upon a time, there was a little black kitten. He came to live with a cute little girl because he was a present for her birthday. He was adorable, everyone thought so, and his little girl loved him very much.

As a kitten, he grew up in a sunny yard that was behind the little girl's house. There were all sorts of things to play with. He would pounce on butterflies, but of course, they were always able to fly away before he got them. He would chase dandelion seeds when the wind blew them. He would stalk ants in the grass though they would dart away. None of that bothered the little black cat because the most fun of all was playing with his girl. She would dangle string, throw little balls and squeaky toys so he could catch them and bring them back. It made him feel quite special that he could have so much fun with his girl. He quickly learned how to purr because he was so happy. In fact, he purred so much that the little girl named him Purr.

As the little girl got older, she made friends with some of the other children in the neighborhood. There were some mean kids in the neighborhood, but the little girl never played with them. All of her friend were nice and polite and lots of fun. They would come over to her house and play in the pretty backyard. They would play tag or hide-and-seek or catch. And they always included Purr. He became friends with all the children and whenever they came to visit he would always, that's right, purr.

Sometimes the little girl would go to her friends' house and play in their yards. Purr was so well behaved and so friendly that he was allowed to go with her. All the other kids and their parents loved Purr. He was having quite the perfect life for a kitten. He was having so much fun that he barely noticed it when he grew up to be a cat.

Being a cat didn't make much difference to Purr. He still felt like a kitten. He still played like a kitten, and of course, he still purred like a kitten only louder. The children didn't treat him any differently either. They still played games and still played with him and he still purred.

Pretty soon the sunny days started to get shorter. The leaves started to change color. The kids started to talk about something called Halloween. Purr didn't know what Halloween was, but the children were all very excited. He listened carefully to what they were saying. They started talking about costumes and something called trick or treat and how many more days they had to wait for Halloween. Purr was quite puzzled.

One day, his girl said, "Purr, I've decided what to be for Halloween. I will be a witch and you will be my scary black cat!" She sounded very excited. She patted Purr on the head, and he purred. She laughed and said, "I will have to teach you to be scary."

Purr wasn't exactly sure what that meant, but he loved his girl, and he would do anything she wanted him to do if he could just figure out what "scary" meant.

The little girl and her friends all decided to get Purr ready for Halloween. They tried on their costumes and paraded in front of Purr, yelling and screaming and trying to show him how to be scary. Purr only purred more.

"Oh goodness," said the little girl. "I don't know if Purr can learn to be scary."

All the kids thought and thought. So did Purr. Then they had an idea. If Purr couldn't be scary, maybe he could just look scary. They put their heads together and came up with a plan. They would make a scary hat for Purr to wear for Halloween. And they did.

They found an old knit cap that they could tie around Purr's head. Then they found feathers on the ground and twigs that were bent and twisted. The final thing they found and added was a blinking light on an old toy wand that someone had. It looked like a blinking eye. They stuck all these things into the knit hat and decided they had made the scariest hat ever. Purr tried it on. It was perfect.

They took Purr with his scary hat over to a mirror. Purr decided that he would make a scary face when he looked into the mirror. He was determined!

They showed Purr the mirror. When he saw his face with the scary hat, he let out the loudest sound he'd ever made, "Purrrrrr!"

The truth was that Purr didn't think he looked scary. He thought he looked pretty funny except for the light which looked like an eye. The hat wasn't that scary. And the kids, when they looked at him with the hat on, started laughing. He did look funny!

"Oh well," said his girl. "It's still a great hat, and it's perfect for Purr to wear on Halloween."

The next night was Halloween. Purr was sorry he couldn't be scary. He tried and tried all day to screech, but the only sound that would come out was a purr. "It's hopeless," he thought.

When the children went out that night to trick or treat, they took Purr with them. His girl was dressed up as a witch, and her friends were ghosts, goblins, jack-o-lanterns, and all sorts of Halloween costumes. Whenever they went to a house, they said in scary voices altogether, "TRICK OR TREAT!" The people in the houses would jump back. Then they would spot Purr, and he would purr. This made the people laugh, and the kids got extra treats.

Then they ran into the mean kids. The mean kids said mean things and tried to take away the little girl's and her friends' treats. One of the mean kids went right up to Purr's girl and said, "Give me your treat bag!"

As he stepped forward, he accidentally stepped on Purr's tail. Without even thinking, Purr screeched. His screech was so loud and so scary that everyone jumped. He screeched and screeched until the mean boy took his foot off Purr's tail. Everyone was shocked! The mean kids looked down and saw a black something, but since it was dark, all they could see was the glowing eye light on Purr's hat. That was enough.

"It's a monster!" they yelled, and off they ran. Purr's girl and her friends started to laugh.

"Well," said Purr's girl, "I guess being scary isn't important after all, Purr. But being scary when we needed you was perfect. You did just the right thing. You scared those mean kids and helped us. We love you, Purr. Thank you!"

"And he got us extra treats!" said one of her friends.

And Purr purred.

THE END

The Beautiful Bunny

Once upon a time there was a little girl bunny who was very, very pretty. Her name was Dolly. Now, as you know, all bunnies are cute, but Dolly was exceptionally pretty. Her ears were a silky gray and just the perfect size and shape. Her face had dazzling white fur, which puffed just right around her cheeks. Her nose was pink, her whiskers were white, and her coat was beautiful. It was a shiny gray-brown that was so soft, and her feet and tail were pure white. All of this made her very adorable, but the one thing that Dolly had that not very many other bunnies had was that her eyes were sparkling blue with very long lashes.

Now from the time she was born, everyone made comments about how pretty Dolly was. Her mommy and daddy were very proud of her since she was so pretty. While Dolly was growing up, she learned how to groom herself so that her ears, face, and coat always looked their best. She learned how to fluff her cheek fur so that when you looked at her, your heart would just melt. While she was growing up, all the other little bunnies would go outside and play. They would run and jump and play tag. They would play hide and seek. They would play leap frog, and believe me, bunnies are the best at leap frog. All the little bunnies got to be good friends. They would ask Dolly to come play with them, but Dolly always said, "No."

"Why not?" they asked.

"I don't want to muss my fur or get dirt on my feet or ears. That's why," Dolly answered.

All the other little bunnies looked at her kind of funny. They didn't say anything. They just went back to playing their games. After a while, they quit asking Dolly to play with them. And Dolly kept grooming her silky ears and her fluffy cheek fur and her perfectly white feet and her shiny coat.

One day, all the little bunnies were old enough to go to school. Their mommies would fix their lunches, which they carried on their backs as they hopped to school. Dolly went to school too. On the first day, she met another little girl bunny whose name was Penny. Penny was cute, as all bunnies are, and she was named Penny because her fur was a pretty shade of red-brown. Even though she was not as pretty as Dolly, they sat right next to each other. Their teacher was a very wise rabbit named Miss Elizabeth.

Miss Elizabeth was very good at teaching and showing the little bunnies how to learn. She was very wise, and all the rabbit parents were glad that their bunnies had Miss Elizabeth for a teacher. Miss Elizabeth explained that during the day, they would have lessons and sometimes partners for their learning work, but that the day would also include time for lunch and recess.

So Dolly and Penny became partners and friends at school.

At recess time, Penny said to Dolly, "Come on. I'll race you outside to play."

"No, I don't want to play outside. I'd rather stay inside and groom myself and read." Dolly replied.

Now Penny thought that this was a little strange, but since she didn't know Dolly very well, she didn't think much of it. So day after day, even though they liked each other, Penny would go play with the other bunnies while Dolly always stayed inside grooming herself.

After a while, Dolly got a little bored because, even though it took her a long time to groom herself, it didn't take all of the recess time so there was time left over. She said to Miss Elizabeth, "I don't see much of the other bunnies except in class. I thought school would be more fun with the other bunnies."

Miss Elizabeth replied, "Dolly, you will have more fun at school once you learn."

"Learn what?" asked Dolly.

But Miss Elizabeth did not answer. Recess was over, and the other bunnies were coming into the classroom to start their lessons again. Miss Elizabeth asked for someone to come to the front of the class to write some math problems on the blackboard. Penny raised her hand. Penny was very good at math. Dolly raised her hand. Miss Elizabeth picked Penny.

Dolly pouted and said, “I should be the one to be at the front of the class because I’m the prettiest bunny.”

Penny said to Miss Elizabeth, “It’s okay. Let Dolly do it.”

Miss Elizabeth looked at Penny and then at Dolly. She said, “Penny, you come up. Dolly, you can come up once you learn.”

“Learn what?” asked a puzzled Dolly.

Miss Elizabeth didn’t answer.

At the end of the class, Miss Elizabeth announced a surprise. The next day, they would be going on a field trip to the Great Meadow and have a picnic lunch. She had asked all the rabbit mommies to send something for their picnics.

The little bunnies were excited! The Great Meadow was quite the most wonderful place in the forest where they lived. It had a special place to play: a pond they could jump into if it was hot enough, flowers to munch on for treats, and a great swing made out of a vine. They couldn't wait!

The next morning, Dolly's mother packed some carrot cake cupcakes carefully in Dolly's backpack for the picnic. Dolly said, "Mom, if I carry my backpack with all that in it, it will mess up my fur."

Dolly's mommy said, "Just this once, Dolly, you need to carry it. The other bunnies are counting on these treats."

Dolly grumbled some more but off she went. As soon as she got to school, she took off the pack and started to groom her fur. Miss Elizabeth told the class to form a line, and she put all the picnic items in a large cart, which two of the daddy rabbits pulled for them. Off they went.

Now to get to the Great Meadow, they had to cross a stream. There were rocks to hop on, so it wasn't too difficult except for Dolly. She was not used to jumping far or back and forth because she never played outside. She was scared to cross the stream. Penny looked at her and said, "Come on. You can do it. Just follow where I hop." She started across the stream.

Dolly watched her and tried very carefully to follow. She hated this! Her feet were getting wet. The rocks were slippery and had mud on them. Yuk! She managed to follow Penny to the second to last rock. When she tried to make that hop, she slipped, went way up in the air, did a somersault, and came down right smack in the water.

She was drenched. She wasn't hurt, but her fur was flat, her feet were muddy, and her ears and cheeks were dripping. She was miserable.

When the other bunnies saw her, they laughed. It was quite a spectacular sight. They knew she wasn't hurt because she immediately hopped to the bank. But she was covered with mud and soaking wet. When she realized the bunnies were laughing at her, she started to cry.

The other bunnies stopped laughing. Penny was the first one to grab a towel, which they brought for swimming in the pond and helped Dolly to dry off. Then all the other bunnies came over to see if they could help. They knew that even though Dolly wasn't hurt, it had to be a very scary experience.

Dolly was surprised. She didn't think the other bunnies liked her very much, and here they were helping her. They gave her a towel to dry off and a washcloth to clean her fur. Penny even helped her fluff her cheek fur!

She looked over, and Miss Elizabeth was watching everything. Miss Elizabeth came over to Dolly and very gently asked her, "Dolly, did you learn something today?"

"Yes, Miss Elizabeth, I think I did," answered Dolly.

What did you learn?" asked Miss Elizabeth.

Dolly thought for a minute and said, "I learned that it's not enough to be pretty on the outside. You have to be pretty on the inside as well. When you help someone and they help you then everyone is a beautiful bunny."

Miss Elizabeth just smiled and the rest of the day was perfect.

THE END

About the Author

Patricia S. Rogers was born and raised in Washington State. She attended Stephens College for two years and then graduated with a Bachelor of Arts in Communications/Advertising from the University of Washington. She worked in Retail until she married and had her two sons. Then she and her husband started a Frozen Specialty Food Distribution business in the state of Oregon.

Patricia helped to run the company with her husband for 25 years, when they sold it and retired. Currently, they live in Arizona and spend a great deal of their time traveling to visit their grandchildren. Patricia is an avid Disney fan and takes her grandchildren to Disneyland at every opportunity. Some say that if she didn't have grandchildren, she would rent them.

Whenever she spent the night with her grandchildren, they would ask for her to tell them a story after the light is turned off. They wanted to hear these stories over and over and finally asked her to write the stories down. And so, "Nana's Little Stories," was born.

CPSIA information can be obtained
at www.ICGtesting.com
Printed in the USA
LVIC04*1625060315
429473LV00015B/57